In the Children's Garden

Carole Lexa Schaefer

Illustrated by

Lynn Pauley

Henry Holt and Company

New York

Henry Holt and Company, Inc.
Publishers since 1866
115 West 18th Street
New York, New York 10011

Henry Holt is a registered
trademark of Henry Holt and Company, Inc.

Published in Canada by Fitzhenry & Whiteside Ltd.,
195 Allstate Parkway, Markham, Ontario L3R 4T8.

Library of Congress Cataloging-in-Publication Data
Schaefer, Carole Lexa.
In the Children's Garden/Carole Lexa Schaefer;
illustrated by Lynn Pauley.
Summary: Children are welcome at an urban garden where
they plant seeds, watch them grow, and enjoy their harvest.
[1. Community gardens—Fiction.   2. Gardening—Fiction.]
I. Pauley, Lynn, ill.   II. Title.
PZ7.S3315In   1994   [E]—dc20   93-15980

ISBN 0-8050-1958-8

First Edition—1994

Printed in the United States of America
on acid-free paper. ∞
1   3   5   7   9   10   8   6   4   2

To Waldo and Stefan,
the two brightest blooms in my garden
—C. L. S.

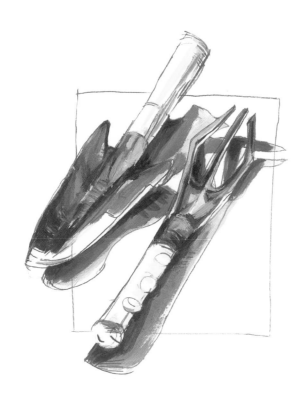

For my family
and that invincible garden
that grows within us all
—L. P.

On an open lot between Old City Park and Maestro Finelli's Music School, there's a garden patch grown by children who live in the neighborhood.

A sign on the garden's gate says
Children's Garden
WELCOME!
That means: Come in, please.
Listen, see, smell, touch—even taste.

In the Children's Garden, deep, dark dirt,
rich with rotted grass, apple peels, and onionskins,
is tunneled through by worms
who wriggle it loose, and give it air—
ah-h-h.

In the Children's Garden, well-worn tools,
rows of spades, rakes, and hoes
are used—*sca-ritch, sca-rutch*—
to turn, to pile, to dig the dirt,
making mounds and holes.

In the Children's Garden, all sorts of seeds—
round brown, plump white, flat black—
are scattered, or dropped one by one,
then covered with dirt by hands that
pat, pat, pat.

In the Children's Garden, boxes, pots, and plots
full of dirt and seeds get soaked by showers
from clouds or hoses, buckets or cans,
so everything stays drip-drop damp—
even under the sizzling sun.

In the Children's Garden, tender sprouts
pop out of soft dirt beds,
slim-stemmed with leaves in twos
—all small—
yet strong enough to stretch their green tops up,
and reach their root toes down.

In the Children's Garden, corn rows, strawberry clumps, pumpkin tangles, lettuce groups, tomato clusters, sunflower stands, zucchini tumbles, and green bean tents grow, forming patterns that fill the spaces with leaves and flowers, vegetables and fruit.

In the Children's Garden, children call:
"Listen to those crows caw and cackle."
"Well, talk back. Tell them to stay out
of our corn."

"Look at the shape of this funny tomato."
"Ha! It's a clown's head with a big red nos
"Smell the spearmint I grew. Rub it with
your fingers."
"Mmm, I like to chew it."

"Whew, pulling weeds is hot, hard work!"
"It's cool in the bean tent. Let's take a rest."

In the Children's Garden, near the gate,
dust-brown children carrying
brimful baskets home
stop a moment to watch
while a sunflower does an evening dance,
nodding its shaggy head,
and rustling its leafy dress.

On the gate, the sign still says
Children's Garden
WELCOME!

That means: Come back to visit anytime,
with one friend or ten. And, if you like,
in your own dirt spot—a yard, a lot,
or even a giant-size flowerpot—
plant another children's garden.